Mystery!

DISCARDED

CELESTA THIESSEN
KEZIAH THIESSEN

CONTENTS

CHAPTER 1 –
DRAGON HABITAT

"Ohhhh..." Princess Keziah groaned for the third time that morning. "This is impossible! How am I supposed to figure out where dragons live?" Keziah had long, curly brown hair and brown eyes. She was wearing one of her lovely, pink princess dresses.

Eight-year-old Keziah was doing a Science project about animals - about their habitats and how they fight. She had chosen dragons and magic night cats for her project. Keziah and her brothers and sisters were all sitting in the Kitty Castle Library, working on their Science projects.

"You could just make it up," said Prince David. David had blonde hair and brown eyes.

"David, this is supposed to be real research. I can't write something that's not true!" said Keziah.

Her five-year-old brother shrugged. "Mr. Raymond, our tutor, doesn't believe in dragons anyway, or magic night cats!" Mr. Raymond was taking care of them while their parents were away on a quest.

Their parents, the king and queen, were trying to find something to use to fight the dragons that had taken over the kingdom.

"I really need the right information," said Keziah.

"We could go take a look," said David.

"Yes," said Priscilla, "we could go explore the dragons' habitat!" Priscilla was Keziah's sister, one of the triplets of Kitty Castle. Their other sister, Celesta, was also nodding enthusiastically. They both had brown eyes. Priscilla had long, straight brown hair and Celesta had long, blond curly hair.

"With Nightcat, of course," said Richard, their older brother. He was eleven and had brown eyes and brown hair.

"Let's talk to him tonight!" Keziah said excitedly.

Nightcat was their pet. But he was no ordinary cat. The children's love had turned him into a magical creature! By night, he was a giant, tiger-like cat with great wings, and he could fly! But, by day, he was a normal, soft grey cat. The children had learned that, if night cats (cats that stay up all night) were treated kindly, they became like their pet, Nightcat. But if people were mean to night cats, they turned into dragons! No one knew how this special magic had come to their kingdom.

"Shh..." said Richard. "Mr. Raymond will be coming to check on our progress."

That night, the children asked Nightcat to help them explore the dragons' habitat.

"I'm not sure that's a good idea," said Nightcat. "It's dangerous out there!"

"I won't do well on my Science project if we don't," Keziah objected.

"You won't get a good mark anyway," said David. "Mr. Raymond won't believe your report."

"But I'll know it's true," said Keziah. "That's what matters."

"I think it would be okay to explore the dragons' habitat," said Richard. "We could use Celesta's cape to makes ourselves invisible!"

"Great idea!" said Celesta. She had received a beautiful, light blue cape for her eighth birthday. The cape had belonged to their Great Aunt Esmeralda. The children had discovered that whoever wore the cape became invisible!

"Wait!" protested Nightcat. "I can only carry three children on my back at one time!"

"Well," said Keziah, "Celesta and Richard didn't get to go when we went over the wall last time, and it's *my* project."

"What about me!?" complained Priscilla. "I didn't get to go last time either."

"There'll be other times," Keziah said to her sister.

"Okay," said Priscilla. "I'll stay home this time, but I want to go next time!"

"Alright," said Richard, "it's settled."

That night, the children began their journey to find the dragons' home. They went out into the castle courtyard. The stars shone in a clear sky and the moon was almost full. Celesta was wearing her blue cape and was invisible!

Nightcat flew down and landed neatly beside them. He had been scouting around outside the castle walls.

"There are not too many dragons out tonight," he said.

"That's good!" said Keziah. "Dragons can't sleep very quietly. Maybe we can follow the sounds of their loud snoring right to their home."

Priscilla giggled.

"Where's Celesta?" asked Nightcat.

"I'm right here!" Celesta laughed and threw off her cape.

"Alright, let's go!" said Nightcat. "Get on my back."

Richard climbed up on the giant cat's back. Then he helped his sisters, Keziah and Celesta, get on too.

"Too bad I can't use my cape now," said Celesta. "It wouldn't fit over Nightcat's wings."

"That's okay," said Richard. "Nightcat can outfly any dragon."

"Ready?" asked Nightcat, as he began to run across the courtyard. He jumped and flapped his great wings. They flew up, up, up, and then over the very high wall. The sky was almost clear of dragons and the stars twinkled brightly. And, sure enough, they *did* hear very loud snoring.

"I believe it's coming from this direction," said Nightcat, veering south.

"Look! What's that?" asked Celesta, pointing into the distance.

"It's a volcano!" Richard said.

"And I think the noise is coming from just that direction!" exclaimed Keziah.

"I don't think that volcano is extinct," said Richard. "I think I see smoke coming out of it."

The children strained to see. There was a little grey smoke coming out of the volcano.

"Don't get too close, Nightcat," said Celesta. "It might be dangerous."

As Nightcat flew farther south, the volcano looked bigger and bigger. The snoring was so loud that Keziah tried to plug her ears, which was pretty difficult since she had to hold on to Nightcat at the same time.

When they got there, Nightcat circled around the volcano.

"What now?" asked Nightcat.

"Let's get a closer look," said Keziah.

"Yeah," said Richard. "Let's go into the volcano. I think it would be safe."

"Yes," said Celesta, "let's go."

"We must be very careful," said Nightcat. "Even if the volcano *is* safe, the dragons aren't. And sometimes dragons can be tricky."

Just as he said the word 'tricky', a black dragon swooped down from above. They had not seen it earlier because the black dragon blended in with the night. All they could see of it, even now, were its glowing eyes. Nightcat dodged the large dragon and dove for the cover of trees below. He flew down into the woods beside the volcano. The dragon didn't follow them down into the woods.

"That was a close one!" said Richard.

"As I said, dragons can be tricky," repeated Nightcat.

Nightcat landed with a thump. The forest was dark.

"Let's be extra careful," said Celesta loudly, to be heard above the dragons' snoring.

"How are we going to get in?" asked Keziah.

"We'll find a way," said Richard.

Carefully, they crept closer to the edge of the volcano. Then they saw something.

A small cave. They didn't see any dragons nearby.

"Maybe there's dragon treasure in there!" exclaimed Richard.

"There's only one way to find out," said Keziah. "Let's go in."

"I don't know," said Celesta. "It looks very dark in there. It might be too dangerous."

"I have my flashlight," said Keziah. "And I made sure to put new batteries in it this time."

"And we can all hide under your cape, Celesta," said Richard, "so it should be okay."

The children and Nightcat all scooted under Celesta's huge cape. "I still can't believe we all fit under here," remarked Celesta.

"I think this cape has grown," said Richard. "It must be more of the magic at work."

Slowly, they walked toward the small cave. Keziah shone her flashlight into the opening.

CHAPTER 2 –
PRISCILLA'S SLIPPERS

As the group moved closer to the cave's entrance, the ground suddenly started slipping away beneath them.

"Ahhhhh!" Celesta screamed!

Then they were sliding down a long, dark tunnel. The loud snoring had stopped. To their horror, the children and Nightcat realized the dragons had just woken up. They must have heard the scream.

Whoosh! The children and Nightcat came out the bottom of the tunnel. Keziah, Celesta, and Richard landed right in a metal cage, and it snapped closed! Nightcat just managed to avoid the trap by flying up into the cavern.

Just then, a huge white dragon swooped down toward Nightcat. Nightcat opened his mouth and breathed sparkle dust at the beast. Instantly, the dragon fell asleep and dropped to the ground with a thud.

"Go get help!" yelled Richard. "Bring the magic water and the magic golden key! Maybe the key will open this cage!"

The golden key had opened Great Aunt Esmeralda's house and also the golden box containing the Book of Answers.

Nightcat didn't want to leave his friends. But more dragons were coming into the cave! Nightcat breathed sparkle dust everywhere as hard as he could. Fifteen more dragons fell asleep and so did the children! Quickly, Nightcat made a decision. He would have to go back to Kitty Castle for the magic water and the golden key.

Nightcat flew back up the tunnel. Then he swooped out of the volcano and up into the night sky. The way back to the castle was much more dangerous because the dragons were awake and chasing him!

He dodged this way and that, breathing sparkle dust everywhere. When he finally made it back to the castle, Priscilla and David were waiting for him in the dark courtyard.

"What happened?" asked David.

"Where are Keziah, Celesta, and Richard?" asked Priscilla.

"They got trapped!" cried Nightcat. "I need help to save them. There were dragons everywhere!"

"We need to get some magic water!" said Priscilla.

"Lots of it!" said David.

"And the golden key," said Nightcat.

"I'll get the key," said David, running back into the castle.

"What can we carry a lot of water in?" asked Nightcat.

They stood and looked at each other for what felt like a long time.

"I don't think we could bring a well," said Nightcat. "What else can hold a lot of water?"

"A rain cloud," suggested Priscilla.

"I don't think we could get the magic water into a rain cloud."

Just then, David returned with the golden key.

"Maybe some of the magic gifts from Great Aunt Esmeralda could help us," suggested Priscilla.

"How 'bout the fuzzy purple slippers? We haven't found out what those do yet!" said David.

Priscilla laughed. "I don't think my slippers will help us carry water."

"I guess we'll just have to use buckets," said Nightcat.

"I'll go get my slippers, just in case they might help."

And, sure enough, when she came back into the courtyard, the slippers were no longer just ordinary slippers.

"Look! They float!" said Priscilla, letting them go. The slippers hovered at her waist, and they glowed purple on the bottom.

"Wow!" said Nightcat. "Look at that! They have small clouds under them. Maybe we will be able to get the magic water into a rain cloud after all!"

"Let's go get the magic water!" said David, excitedly.

They walked back into the castle, past the kitchen and down the stairs into the secret passageway. They hurried along the dark tunnel. Nightcat led the way because he could see in the dark. The children put their hands on his back so they would know which way to go and so they wouldn't bump into anything. Nightcat led them to the room that held the lake of magic water.

"Remember," said Nightcat, "don't touch the water or you will turn into a kitten."

Carefully, Priscilla set her purple fuzzy slippers on top of the water. The slippers began to gather the magic water into huge purplish clouds beneath them.

"I think we just found out what your slippers do," said David.

"Those slippers won't fit my paws," said Nightcat. "Priscilla, I think you will need to come with me."

"Of course. They're my slippers. I want to wear them."

"I want to come too," said David.

"The other three children are still at the volcano. I wouldn't be able to carry the four of you back."

"Awww! I really want to go! I want to help."

"Maybe I can carry you," said Priscilla. "Let's go up to the courtyard and try it."

Without touching the water, Priscilla picked up her slippers.

"What if I touch the cloud?" asked Priscilla.

"I don't know. But I think you'd better not," said Nightcat.

Together, they walked through the secret passage. Then David ran ahead. Soon, they heard a loud thump.

"Ouch!" cried David. Dust was everywhere.

"What happened?" asked Priscilla.

"I bumped into a post," said David.

Then they heard a loud crack.

"Let's hurry," said Nightcat.

A moment later, they were up the stairs and out of the secret passageway. Once they had reached the courtyard, Priscilla carefully put on the slippers. Slowly, she began to float up into the dark, star-filled sky.

"Wait for me!" cried David.

"Come back!" called Nightcat.

"I can't control it!" said Priscilla.

"Try walking!" said David.

Priscilla tried walking. She did move forward but she kept floating up.

"Walk like you're coming down stairs," called Nightcat.

Priscilla tried walking like she was coming down stairs. It worked! Slowly, she walked down to them.

"Now you know how to control it," said Nightcat.

"I wonder if it would work with only one slipper," said David.

"I don't think so, David," said Priscilla. "But you could stand on my feet and hold on to me."

"What?!" said David.

Priscilla showed him what she meant.

"I think it would be really hard for you to walk with David standing on your feet," said Nightcat.

"I could give you a piggyback ride," said Priscilla.

"Let's just go," said Nightcat. "We need to hurry up. The other children are in danger! And we've taken too long already. Get on my back, David."

David climbed on and Nightcat ran across the courtyard. Then he jumped into the air and flapped his huge wings. They were off in no time. The moon was high in the sky, giving soft white light to the world below. When they got over the castle wall, they were relieved to find the dragons had decided to return home and go back to sleep. Loud snoring could be heard coming from the volcano once more.

Nightcat flew as quickly as he could. Priscilla had to run in her cloud slippers to keep up. When they got there, Nightcat flew down to the bottom of the volcano and found the cave. Priscilla was right behind him, running like she was running down stairs. She was tired from running so far. Very loud snoring was coming from the cave.

"We're going in there?" asked Priscilla.

"We have to," said Nightcat. "That's where the other children are."

CHAPTER 3 – CHARCOAL

The group entered the dark cave. When they got to the back of it, they saw sleeping dragons all around a large, metal cage. Keziah's flashlight was still shining. The cage held more than just the sleeping children. In the cage slept a very large cat with wings.

"Another Nightcat!?" cried Priscilla and David at the same time.

"He looks just like you," said Priscilla.

Nightcat landed beside the cage.

"Quick, David, use the key."

"But Nightcat, there's another Nightcat in there."

"It's not a dragon," said Nightcat, "so we know it's a good creature. We don't have to be afraid."

"We need to bring it back to Kitty Castle," said David.

"But they're all still asleep," said Priscilla.

"Not for long," said Nightcat. "They're waking up."

"What about the dragons?" asked David.

"Don't worry," said Nightcat. "They're fast asleep. Let's just be very quiet."

David tried the key in the cage door. It worked! He unlocked the door and opened it.

"He does look a lot like me," said Nightcat quietly, looking at the other cat.

Soon the children woke up.

"What's going on?" asked Keziah.

"Nightcat's saving us, that's what," said Richard.

"No, look behind you," said Keziah, pointing at the other huge cat.

Richard tuned to see an exact copy of Nightcat. He was just waking up too!

"Let's figure this out later!" said Nightcat. "Come on. Let's go."

Celesta and Richard climbed up beside David on Nightcat's back. Celesta made sure she had her cape with her. Priscilla walked around the cavern, in the air. Her slippers rained magic water down onto the sleeping dragons. They all turned into kittens and kept sleeping.

"I see you found out what Priscilla's slippers do," remarked Richard.

"That's awesome!" said Celesta. "Now we have another way to fight the dragons."

"We have to go now," urged Nightcat.

"I can carry you," said the other cat to Keziah.

"Okay," said Keziah, climbing up on his back.

Nightcat flew through the tunnel and up into the sky. Priscilla ran behind him. The other giant cat followed them.

"I'm getting tired," gasped Priscilla.

As they headed back to Kitty Castle, Keziah asked the cat she was riding on why he looked exactly like Nightcat.

"I'll explain everything when we get back to Kitty Castle," he said softly.

The starry sky was clear as they flew toward to the castle. Priscilla had to run to keep up with the two, flying night cats but they made sure not to leave her behind. When they reached the castle, the giant cats landed in the courtyard. The children got off the big cats' backs. The cats looked at each other in the moonlight.

"Who are you?" Nightcat asked the other cat.

"I'm your father."

The children gasped.

"My father?" asked Nightcat.

"Yes. I was with my owner, Great Aunt Esmeralda, and with Mist. I stayed back to fight the dragons so that they could get away. We were looking for something that would get rid of the dragons forever."

"Who's Mist?" asked Keziah.

"Nightcat's mother."

The children gasped again.

"Where are they now?" asked Priscilla.

"I don't know."

"Father!" said Nightcat. "I missed you! I never knew you turned into a magic night cat too!"

Nightcat and his father nuzzled each other and then his father licked him.

"What should we call you?" asked Celesta.

"My name is Charcoal."

All the children greeted Charcoal by name and petted the newest member of the family.

"When the dragons first appeared in the land, Great Aunt Esmeralda got very worried," explained Charcoal. "She knew from the Book of Answers that there was only one way to get rid of the dragons forever. She needed the golden kitten statue. But she didn't know where it was."

"I have that statue!" Richard exclaimed. "We found it the courtyard when we were making a garden." He pulled a small, golden kitten statue from his pocket.

"That's wonderful news," said Charcoal.

"But now we need Great Aunt Esmeralda back," said Nightcat.

"We also need to find the golden flute," said Charcoal. "A dragon swiped it when Great Aunt Esmeralda was bringing some things to Kitty Castle for safe-keeping."

"What happened to Great Aunt Esmeralda?" asked Celesta.

"We chased the dragon with the golden flute into the volcano but there were many dragons there and they began attacking us. Then we saw the dragon with the golden flute fly out again. I stayed back to fight the dragons so Great Aunt Esmeralda and Mist could get away and chase the dragon with the golden flute. But, then, I got trapped in that cage. I never saw Great Aunt Esmeralda or Nightcat's mother again."

"How long were you trapped in that cage?" asked Keziah.

"A long time. I don't how long it's been."

"We have the flute too!" cried David, pulling a shiny golden flute from his pocket.

"Where did you find it?" asked Charcoal.

"In a tunnel in the castle wall," said David. "A dragon dug through the castle wall and, when we looking for Mr. Raymond, I went into the tunnel and that's where I found the flute."

"But where *are* Great Aunt Esmeralda and Mist?" asked Celesta.

Charcoal looked sad. "I will have to search for them."

"Wait! Where's the golden key?" asked Nightcat.

CHAPTER 4 – OH, NO!

They all looked at each other. Where *was* the golden key?

"Everyone, check your pockets," suggested Richard.

"I don't have pockets," said Charcoal.

The children giggled.

"This is serious," said Nightcat. "I think we still need that key. It's a very important key. Great Aunt Esmeralda told me to take very good care of it!"

"And now we lost it!" said David. "And it's all my fault. I lost it!"

"It's okay," said Keziah. "We'll just go back and get it. It's still the middle of the night. The dragons will be sleeping."

"Yes," said Nightcat, "we must go back."

"Okay," said Charcoal. "Kids, get on our backs again!"

"What about me?" asked Priscilla.

"You'll have to run," said David.

"Aww...I'm tired."

"I'll wear the slippers," said Keziah.

"No. It's okay. I'm not that tired."

Keziah and Richard rode on Charcoal's back, and David and Celesta rode on Nightcat. The two giant cats and Priscilla rose up into the air.

"Giddy up!" said David.

"Giddy up!" said Keziah.

The children laughed as they began their journey back to the volcano. The moon was setting but the sky was still dark and full of stars.

When they got to the volcano, they saw thick black smoke coming out of its top!

"Oh, no!" cried David.

"Do you think the volcano is going to erupt?" asked Priscilla.

"I don't know," said Charcoal, "but we have to get the key and fast!"

They dove into the passageway at the bottom of the volcano. The kittens were gone. The cavern was empty.

"Hurry, find the key," cried Richard, as he jumped off Charcoal's back and started looking around on the ground. The other children started looking too.

"Wait!" cried Keziah. "Did we take it out of the cage?"

The cavern was filling with smoke and getting very hot.

"Priscilla, go out already," said Nightcat. "It's getting too dangerous in here!"

"Nightcat," said Charcoal, "take as many children as you can carry and go out too. I'll stay back to find the key."

"You all go," said Keziah. "I'll stay with Charcoal."

David, Richard, and Celesta jumped on Nightcat's back. Then Nightcat flew quickly up the passage after Priscilla.

"Here it is!" cried Keziah. She held up the golden key. "Let's go!" she said, jumping on Charcoal's back.

Charcoal leapt up into the air and flew into the passage. It was very hot, and black smoke was everywhere. They made it out just before the tunnel collapsed.

"Let's fly home!" Keziah cried.

There were dragons swarming everywhere, and the smoke was so thick in the night sky that the children and the cats could hardly see. The dragons were getting very close to them. Everyone was afraid that there might be a mid-air collision. Suddenly, rain started falling from Priscilla's slippers. The dragons that got hit with the drops flew down to the forest below and turned into kittens. The two giant cats flew above Priscilla so the magic water wouldn't drip on them.

Suddenly, there was a huge explosion. Rock and dust flew through the air.

"Hurry!" cried all the children.

"We have to get away," said David.

The night cats flew as fast as they could, and Priscilla ran like she was in a race. Rain continued to fall from the clouds under her slippers.

"Everyone, hold your breath," said Keziah. "Volcanoes give off poisonous gasses."

As they flew through the air toward Kitty Castle, they held their breath for as long as they could. When they couldn't hold their breath any longer, they breathed in, and the air smelled bad.

"Ewww! Rotten eggs!" said David.

"It's not rotten eggs," said Celesta. "It's sulphur from the volcano."

Finally, they made it back home. They landed in the courtyard just as the sun was beginning to rise. The pink clouds looked like cotton candy.

"I'm so tired," said Celesta.

"We just missed a whole night's sleep," said Keziah.

"Let's go to bed now," said Richard. "Maybe Daisy will let us sleep in." Daisy was their cook and was helping to take care of them while their parents were away.

"Wait!" cried Keziah. "Charcoal can't turn into a normal cat during the day, can he?"

They all looked at Nightcat's father.

"No. I can't turn back into a normal cat. How do you do that?"

"I'll go with Charcoal and Nightcat into the secret passageway while the rest of you get to bed," volunteered Keziah.

"I'll come too," said Richard.

"Wait," said Priscilla. "What should I do with my slippers? I can't wear them to bed."

Everyone looked at her fuzzy purple slippers, with the light purple clouds glowing underneath them.

"We shouldn't put them anywhere where Mr. Raymond or Daisy could touch them," said Keziah.

"Right," said Priscilla. "We don't want any more kittens *that* way."

"What about in a big box?" suggested Celesta.

"Do you think the water would leak through the box?" asked Richard.

"Probably," said Priscilla.

"What holds water but doesn't leak?" asked Keziah.

"I know," said David. "Two pails!"

"That's a good idea," said Nightcat. "We could put boards over top so the slippers don't float out."

"Right! I'll get the pails," said David.

"I'll get the boards," said Celesta.

So Keziah and Richard led Charcoal into the secret passageway while the rest of the children stayed in the courtyard to finish putting Priscilla's slippers away.

"We had better hurry," said Richard. "Daisy would be pretty shocked to see *two* magic night cats."

"Yes. We need to explain it to her first," Keziah agreed.

They entered the dark passageway that led down from the kitchen. Keziah pulled out her flashlight and turned it on. The yellow beam shone on a large pile of stones blocking the passageway.

"Oh, no!" said Nightcat. "There's been a cave-in!"

CHAPTER 5 – DEPARTURE

"Let's try to take the passageway from the library," suggested Richard.

They walked through the kitchen. Keziah stopped to pet their kittens, Surprise and Sushi, who were curled up, asleep, near the fireplace. The other children were coming in from the courtyard with two buckets, covered by boards. The buckets were floating up.

Priscilla had to struggle to hold them down.

"That was quick," said David to Charcoal.

"There was a cave-in," Keziah explained. "We couldn't get to the water."

"We're going to try the secret passage from the library," said Richard. So Richard, Keziah, Charcoal, and Nightcat hurried to the library.

"Where should I put these pails?" asked Priscilla. "They're floating away!"

"We should find something heavy to put them under," said Celesta.

"Hmm...We could try to putting them under the piano!" said David.

"Wouldn't that squish them?" asked Priscilla.

"What else could we put them under?" asked Celesta.

"We could hide them in the top of my closet," suggested Priscilla.

Meanwhile, in the library, Keziah and Richard had found that they couldn't get through from there either.

"The cave-in must have happened where all the passages meet. We'll have to dig through," said Keziah.

The children tried to push the stones off the pile. Dust rained down.

"This is too dangerous," said Charcoal. "Nightcat and I could probably dig through, but the passages are unstable. They could collapse again while we're working."

"I know where we could get some of the magic water!" exclaimed Richard. "Priscilla's slippers! I'm sure there's still some magic water left in the clouds there."

"Good idea!" said Nightcat. "We'll have to figure out how to fix these passageways later."

They walked slowly back to the children's rooms. Then Keziah noticed the color of the sky outside the high windows. "It's almost full daylight! We have to get to bed!"

When they got into the room, the other children were already in bed.

"Where are your slippers, Priscilla?" asked Nightcat. "We need that magic water."

"They're here," she said, as she hurried to her closet and opened the door. Up at the top of her closet floated two buckets. "I can't reach them," said Priscilla.

"I can," said Nightcat, flapping his wings. Carefully, he caught one bucket and brought it down to the floor. He nudged the board off the top with his nose. Priscilla grabbed the slipper so it didn't float up and rain on all of them.

"Dad," Nightcat said, "you need to take one lick of the magic water. No more and no less."

"Okay," said Charcoal. Priscilla held up the slipper and he took a lick of the rain from underneath.

Slowly, Charcoal and Nightcat turned into normal grey cats as sunlight came into the room.

Keziah and Richard jumped into their beds. Priscilla slammed the board back down on the slipper, pushed the bucket into the closet, closed the door, and leapt into bed too.

They were almost asleep when they heard Daisy calling.

"Time for breakfast, Children!"

"We didn't even get a minute of sleep," said Keziah, as she got out of bed.

"Oh, well, it's okay," said David. "I'm starving anyway!"

"And I do have to finish my Science project," said Keziah. "Now I know just where the dragons live. In a volcano filled with traps. And the volcano isn't extinct!"

***

That night, under the light of a full moon, Charcoal said goodbye to the children and Nightcat.

"Do you really have to leave?" asked Keziah. "We just found you!"

"I have to go and find Mist and Great Aunt Esmeralda."

"How will you know where to look?" asked Priscilla.

"What if they're dead?" asked David.

"David!" cried the girls.

"But what if they are? They never found the golden flute."

"I just know Mist is alive," said Charcoal. "I can feel it."

"Something must have happened to them," said Richard, "or Great Aunt Esmeralda would have come back to her house. She would never have left all her cats alone."

"I know I'll be able to find them," said Charcoal. "And when I bring Great Aunt Esmeralda back, she'll be able to use the golden kitten statue and the flute to get rid of the dragons forever."

"Dad! I wish you didn't have to go," said Nightcat. He nuzzled his father. "I love you, Dad."

"I love you, too, Nightcat. I'll find your mother and I'll come back."

All the children hugged Charcoal. Then he flapped his powerful wings and flew up into the starry sky. He circled the courtyard once and then flew over the courtyard wall. The children watched until he was out of sight.

KITTY CASTLE BOOKS

Get all the Kitty Castle books on Amazon.com!

KITTY CASTLE 1 - NIGHTCAT

KITTY CASTLE 2 - SURPRISES!

KITTY CASTLE 3 - ANSWERS!

KITTY CASTLE 4 - MYSTERY!

KITTY CASTLE 5 – REUNION

KITTY CASTLE 6 - CELEBRATIONS

If you liked this book, please leave us a great review on Amazon.com! Thanks for reading!